MAKER

STUDIO

Fun science & tech projects for young designers!

Zoe Bateman & Dr Alison Buxton

THIS IS A WELBECK CHILDREN'S BOOK

Published in 2020 by Welbeck Children's Books

An Imprint of Welbeck Children's Limited, part of Welbeck Publishing Group.

20 Mortimer Street London W1T 3JW

Text & Illustrations © Welbeck Children's Limited, part of Welbeck Publishing Group.

A CIP catalogue record for this book is available from the British Library.

ISBN: 978 1 78312 548 7

Printed in China

10 9 8 7 6 5 4 3 2 1

Writers: Zoe Bateman and Dr Alison Buxton
Design Manager: Matt Drew
Design: Sam James and Andrew Thomas
Editorial Manager: Joff Brown
Production: Nicola Davey
Photographer: Simon Anning
Models: Zoe Bateman, Ravina Patel, Sze Kiu Yeung

The publishers would like to thank the following sources for their kind permission to reproduce the pictures in this book.

SHUTTERSTOCK: A-Star, Ahmet Misirligul, AKKHARAT JARUSILAWONG, Aleksandr Makarenko, alexei_tm, Alexey Boldin, Andrea Danti, Andrey Eremin, chonticha stocker, DenisDavidoff, dibrova, Dmitri Ma, donatas1205, Eddie Jordan Photos, elRoce, Evgeniy Kalinovskiy, focal point, FotoKina, Frank Cornelissen, indigolotos, Ioan Panaite, kryzhov, LeManna, LifetimeStock, Lotus_studio, Madlen, MARLIL, Mihai_Andritoiu, Nasky, pisaphotography, prisma, Rob kemp, SFIO CRACHO, Sinisa Botas, sirastock, SKUpics, StudioSmart, Vector_creator, VICUSCHKA, Viktoriya, Vitaly Korovin, Vladimir Gjorgiev, Walter Bilotta, Yahdi Bin Rus, Yein Jeon, Yellow Cat, Yuri Turkov

Every effort has been made to acknowledge correctly and contact the source and/or copyright holder of each picture any unintentional errors or omissions will be corrected in future editions of this book.

MAKER

STUDIO

Fun science & tech projects for young designers!

WELBECK

Contents

Introduction

Welcome all budding makers! In this book you will learn to make a whole range of different projects, as well as learning more about the science behind how they work. Learn to cast with resin, mix up chemicals to create colour changing bath bombs, or stitch yourself a light-up bag! Remember the main aim is to have fun and to experiment – these instructions are just a guide to help you get started. We encourage you to be creative, try using different materials, and combine the techniques and skills you learn in this book, because that's what being a maker is all about!

About The Authors

Zoe Bateman is a multi-crafter, working with yarn, paper, fabric, and more, who loves nothing better than making things with her hands. She has published several craft books, as well as creating craft tutorials for magazines and websites, consulting on craft-based TV programmes, and teaching workshops to kids and adults around the UK.

Dr Alison Buxton is a maker-educator based in the UK. With over 17 years' experience in STEM/STEAM outreach, she founded the non-profit organisation STEAM Works in 2014 and currently works as a consultant at MakerEd UK and as a part-time educational makerspace developer at the University of Sheffield. Follow her on Twitter at @MakerEdUK.

Tools for the job

These are the some of the most important tools that any maker can use. How many do you have?

Jewellery Pliers

- Jewellery pliers are really useful for fine or fiddly work with wires and small objects like beads or gems.

- Cutting pliers are used for cutting through thin metal such as chain.

- Flat nosed jewellery pliers are used to hold jewellery components while you're working.

- Round nosed jewellery pliers are useful for bending and shaping metal.

⚠ THINK SAFE

Jewellery pliers can be quite sharp and exert a lot of cutting force, so make sure you watch your fingers.

Junior hacksaw

- A junior hacksaw has a fine blade, making it ideal for cutting plastic or even very thin metal.

- The blades can wear down quickly, but they're replaceable.

- For extra stability, clamp the element you're cutting and use two hands on the saw - one on the handle and one on the top of the frame.

- When sawing, press down firmly and use small, pushing strokes.

⚠ THINK SAFE

Be careful when replacing the blade on a junior hacksaw. The teeth should always be pointing away from the handle, and never force the blade into place.

Bradawl

- This hand tool is a bit like a screwdriver, but with a sharp point.

- It is used for making pilot holes for screws, but also very useful for making holes in card and foam.

⚠ THINK SAFE

The sharp point is great for making holes, but keep your hands clear! Use a board or blob of putty behind your material to stop the bradawl scratching your worktop.

SAFETY RATING

Low risk - stay safe by using the tool for the job it is designed for.

Medium risk - always store tools safely and put them away when you are done.

High risk - these tools must be used with great care. If you are unsure how to use it, ask!

Hot glue gun

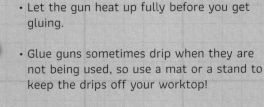

- Let the gun heat up fully before you get gluing.

- Glue guns sometimes drip when they are not being used, so use a mat or a stand to keep the drips off your worktop!

- Don't use too much glue as it can drip onto other parts of your model.

- Always have some spare glue sticks close at hand for when you run out.

⚠ THINK SAFE

The metal tip on a glue gun can get quite hot. Keep your fingers well away from the nozzle!

Craft or precision knife

- These are knives with super sharp blades and great care needs to be taken with them.

- They are best used to cut really straight pieces of paper, card or duct tape.

⚠ THINK SAFE

Always use a cutting mat and raised steel ruler as a guide on a flat surface.
Store your knife in a safe place.
If the blade doesn't have a cover, you can use a cork or lump of modelling clay to cover the sharp bit.

Scissors

- You'll need a large strong pair for cutting through thick materials, and a smaller pair with a pointed end for cutting detailed shapes.

- Keep your scissors sharp by regularly using a sharpening tool on the blades.

- Use the point of your scissors to create holes, and the closed blades to score lines for crisp folds.

- If you get glue or tape on your scissors, you can use a little nail varnish remover to help get rid of the stickiness.

⚠ THINK SAFE

Scissors blades are sharp, especially good quality ones.
Make sure you store scissors with the blades closed.

Ruler

- Use your ruler to measure accurately, and to help draw and cut nice straight lines to give your project a professional finish.

- Try and buy a ruler that has centimetres and inches on, so you are able to measure both as needed.

- If you are using your ruler with a craft knife to cut, try and get a metal ruler as this is much tougher – your knife can cut into a wooden or plastic ruler.

⚠ THINK SAFE

When using a metal ruler to cut with a craft knife, cut slowly and evenly, and make sure your fingers are out of the way.

Hand drills and bits

- These have interchangeable ends of different sizes and for different materials called 'bits'.

- Choose the size of the bit you need based on how big you want your hole.

- Turn the handle clockwise to drill into wood, foam, plastic and metal.

⚠ THINK SAFE

Secure the item you are drilling in a vice to make sure it doesn't slip. Use a bradawl to make a pilot hole to help get you started.

Your Maker kit

Makers are always collecting useful stuff they can use on projects. Here are some essentials!

Coloured card

Colourful sheets of card are perfect for constructing and decorating projects. Card comes in different thicknesses which is measured in gsm (grammes per square metre). The higher the number, the thicker the card will be – so 300gsm will be thicker than 240gsm. To make your card shapes more sturdy, cut out two identical shapes and stick them together.

Cardboard

Cardboard is very strong but can be easily cut, making it ideal for craft projects. Thicker cardboard is called 'double wall' because it is made up of two layers, whereas thinner cardboard is called 'single wall.'

Aluminium wire

Aluminium wire can be easily cut with jewellery pliers or sharp scissors, and can be bent into shape just using your hands or with a pair of flat nosed pliers.

Zip ties

These small plastic ties are a good way of connecting lengths of materials together.

Glue

PVA glue is great for sticking paper and card, but isn't strong enough to hold together heavier materials like wood and metal. Wood glue works well on wood, but is very thick, so isn't good for sticking card.

Tape

It's important to choose the right tape for the job. Packing tape is wide and great for sticking things together more permanently. Masking tape is designed to be removable, so is perfect for a temporary hold, and can be used to give straight lines when painting or to mark a cut line. Double sided tape can be used when you don't want your tape to be visible.

Acrylic Paint

Acrylic paint will stick to lots of different surfaces, so is ideal for creative projects. It's available in lots of different colours, and you can mix colours together to create your own unique shade.

Bamboo skewers, craft sticks & dowels

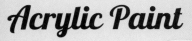

Don't have any wooden dowels? Bamboo skewers are a great alternative. They are pointed at one end, so they can also be used to pierce holes on card and foam.

Staying safe

Safety comes first for any maker. Follow these rules to make sure you're safe!

Dress right

Roll up your sleeves and tie back long hair.

An apron with a pocket will protect your clothes and give you somewhere to store your spare screws!

Work gloves are great to help protect you from minor cuts and glue gun burns.

Protect your eyes

Just like you wouldn't ride in a car without a seatbelt, it is important to always wear goggles when using tools. If you find goggles a bit uncomfortable, try protective glasses instead.

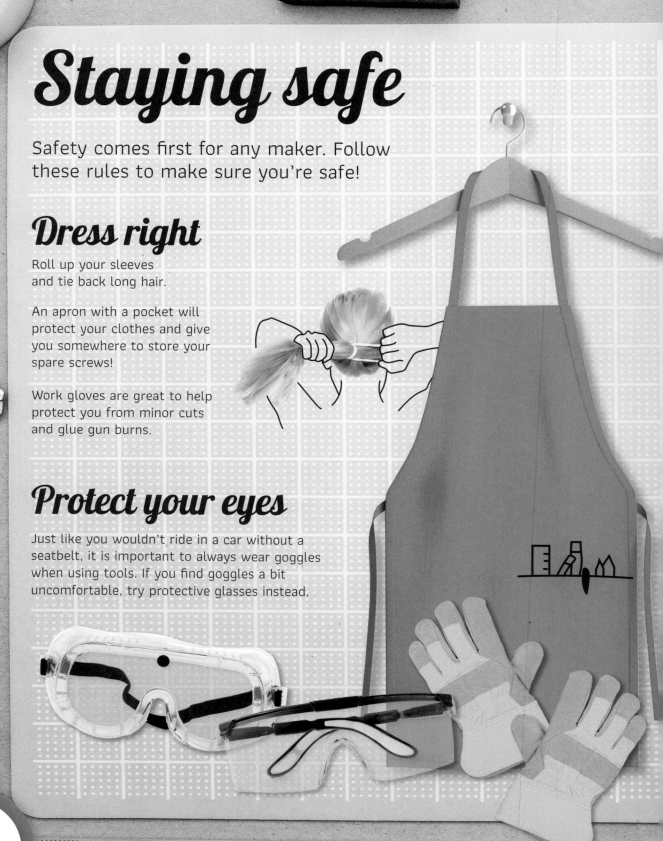

Carry tools correctly

Be aware of who is around you and where you are taking your tools.

It is best to keep smaller tools such as screwdrivers and wires together in a small toolbox.

Point sharp bits down towards the floor.

Need adult supervision?

As you work through the projects, keep an eye out for this badge. Tools are safe if handled correctly, but it's always best to ask an adult to help out with tricky jobs.

Ask an adult to help!

Set up your workspace

Before you begin your project, check your working area is clear and set at a good working height with plenty of room for all of your supplies and tools.

Avoid ⚠ distractions

Try to find a quiet place to work so you can stay focused on the job at hand. A slip in focus might lead to a serious injury to you or someone else.

Right tool for the job

Always use the correct tool for the job you are trying to do.

It can be dangerous to try to use a tool for something it wasn't designed to do.

Becoming a maker

Most makers as well as designers, engineers and other creative folk follow a process like this when doing any project.

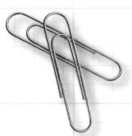

Even when following instructions, things don't always go to plan.

As you progress, you might think of a way to improve a design or model.

The Maker Cycle gives you a framework to get you started, develop your ideas, make and test your design...

...and most importantly, see how you could improve it.

The Maker Cycle

Ask — what do you want to make or improve

Research — what have other people done

Imagine — what yours could look like

Plan — your tools and methods

Make — something awesome

Test — to see if it needs improvements

Sound & Vision

Amazing objects that provide a sound
and light show – without needing
extra electricity!

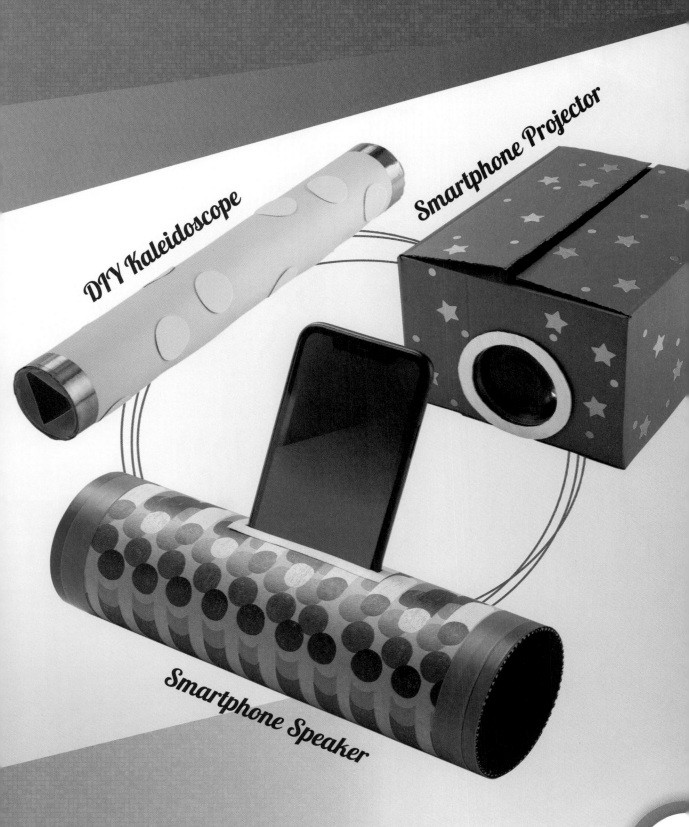

DIY Kaleidoscope

Smartphone Projector

Smartphone Speaker

DIY Kaleidoscope

This kaleidoscope shows how the power of optics and reflection can transform any shape into a complex pattern. Plus it's fun and easy to make!

You will need...

Scissors

Long cardboard tube

Transparent coloured plastic beads

Clear acetate sheets, coloured card and mirrored card

Plus...

- Permanent marker pen
- Glue gun
- Ruler
- Pencil
- Scissors
- Coloured card or paints to decorate

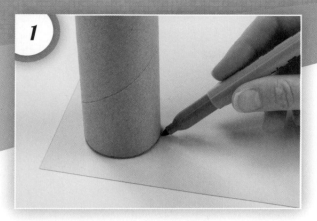

Draw around the end of your cardboard tube onto the acetate using your permanent marker. Repeat this three times, so you have three circles.

Cut out the circles from your acetate, and trim down one circle slightly, so it is just small enough to just fit inside your cardboard tube.

Use a glue gun to glue one of the bigger acetate circles to the end of your tube. Make sure the glue has set before moving to the next stage.

Pour a small handful of the coloured beads into your tube from the opposite end. You need just enough beads to cover the base of the tube.

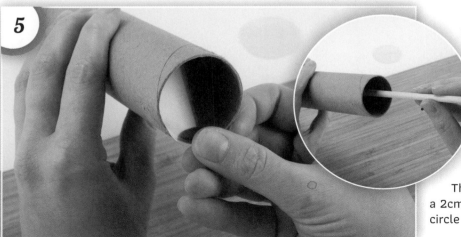

Insert your smaller acetate circle into the tube, and push down to the end using a ruler or something similar. Don't push it right up against the beads, as you want them to have room to move about. There should be around a 2cm gap between the first circle and the second one.

6 Cut a 9cm wide strip of mirrored card a few centimetres shorter than your tube's length. Mark a line at 3cm and 6cm on the back, as shown.

7 Using closed scissors, score along the lines you drew, and then crease along them, folding the card so that the mirrored surface is on the inside.

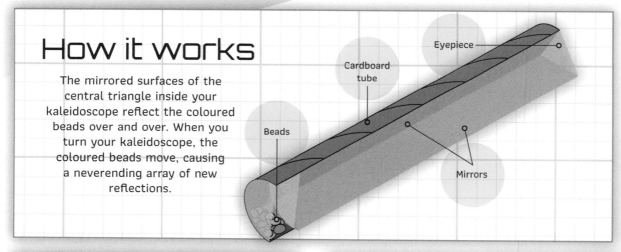

How it works

The mirrored surfaces of the central triangle inside your kaleidoscope reflect the coloured beads over and over. When you turn your kaleidoscope, the coloured beads move, causing a neverending array of new reflections.

Beads

Cardboard tube

Eyepiece

Mirrors

8 You should have a long triangular-shaped card tube now. Carefully glue the two edges together so the triangular tube holds its shape.

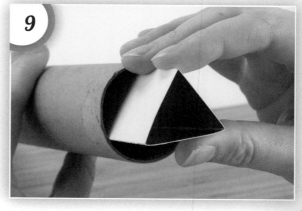

9 Insert your mirrored card into the tube until it just touches the acetate. Don't push down on the acetate or the beads won't be able to move!

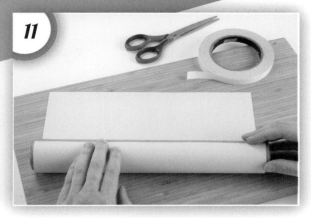

Cut back any mirrored card that's sticking out, then glue your final acetate circle to the tube. This will be the end you look through.

Look into your kaleidoscope near a bright light source, and twist it to see the patterns change. Now decorate it in your own unique style.

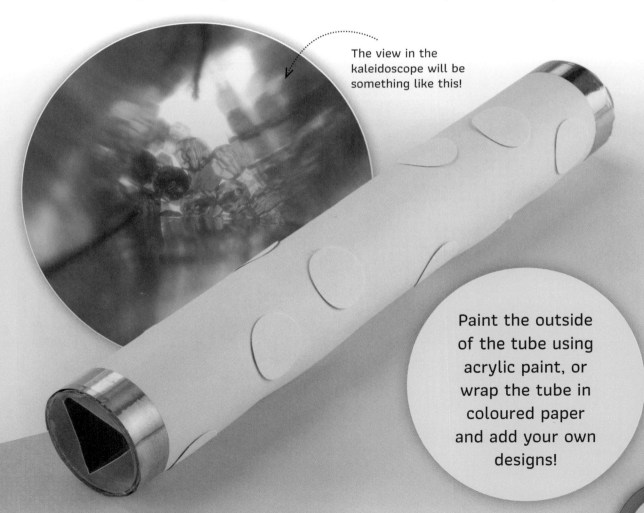

The view in the kaleidoscope will be something like this!

Paint the outside of the tube using acrylic paint, or wrap the tube in coloured paper and add your own designs!

Smartphone Speaker

This phone accessory uses aucoustic engineering to amplify your phone without any electronics – plus it's fun to customize!

You will need...

Cardboard tube

Smartphone

Wrapping paper

Pair of tights

Coloured tape for decoration

Craft sticks

Plus...

- Craft knife
- Marker pen & coloured pens
- Scissors
- Double sided & sticky tape
- Hot glue gun or strong glue

1

Ask an adult to help!

Cut the bottom of your tube off with a craft knife, and remove the lid, so it's open at both ends.

2

Draw a rectangle in the centre of the tube, just big enough to slide your phone in.

3

Ask an adult to help!

Cut out this rectangle with a craft knife, and check that your phone will fit into it.

4

Turn the tube a quarter-turn, then draw a 15mm circle in the middle, and two lines 20cm to each side. Cut them out with a craft knife.

5

Cut the feet off the tights, so you have two 'socks' measuring 100mm.

6

Tie the closed ends of the 'socks' together securely with a double knot.

How it works

Your smartphone amplifier doesn't really increase
the volume of your phone's audio very much.
It actually directs it, so that no sound is lost.

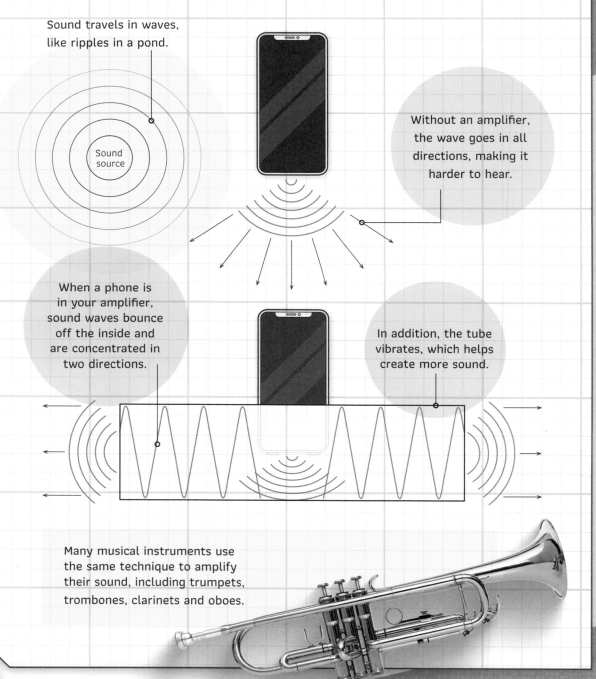

Sound travels in waves,
like ripples in a pond.

Sound source

Without an amplifier,
the wave goes in all
directions, making it
harder to hear.

When a phone is
in your amplifier,
sound waves bounce
off the inside and
are concentrated in
two directions.

In addition, the tube
vibrates, which helps
create more sound.

Many musical instruments use
the same technique to amplify
their sound, including trumpets,
trombones, clarinets and oboes.

When you're sure they're tight, trim off any excess material with a pair of scissors.

Cut two 250mm lengths of double-sided sticky tape, and stick each one 60mm from each end.

Peel off the other side of the sticky tape, then stretch the tights over each end of the tube. Secure them in place with the tape.

Cut off any excess material with scissors.

Cut out a piece of 280mm x 250mm paper for the outer surface. Add two strips of double-sided tape to each end, then wrap tightly around the tube.

Ask an adult to help!

Feel for the holes and slits underneath the paper, then carefully cut matching holes through them with a craft knife.

Cut both ends off two craft stick, to make two 40mm sticks.

Colour the short sticks in with pens or paint, then colour two full-sized craft sticks too.

Insert the full-length sticks into the two slots either side of the small hole.

Use a glue gun to glue the two smaller sticks to the top and bottom of the longer sticks.

Thread your power cable through the hole, and out the slit on the top of your amplifier.

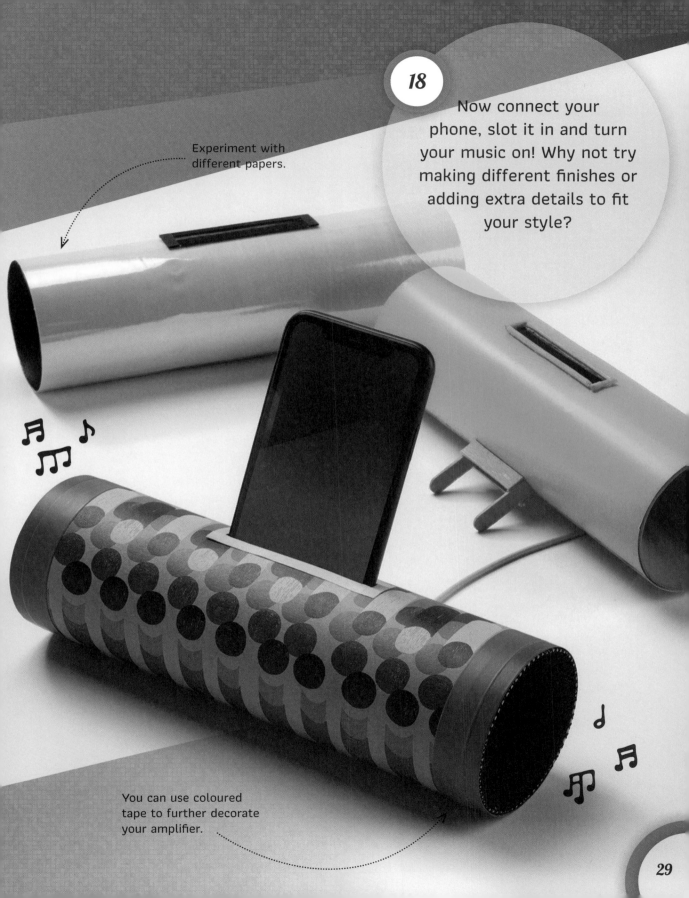

Experiment with different papers.

18 Now connect your phone, slot it in and turn your music on! Why not try making different finishes or adding extra details to fit your style?

You can use coloured tape to further decorate your amplifier.

Smartphone Projector

You will need...

Impress your friends with a homemade projector that projects photos and videos from your smartphone.

10cm magnifying glass with at least 5x magnification

Black acrylic paint and paintbrush

2mm aluminium wire (approximately 50cm)

Empty cardboard box (a shoebox is the perfect size and shape for this project – just make sure your box is taller than the width of your magnifying glass.)

Smartphone

Plus...

- Craft knife
- Pencil
- Glue gun
- Coloured acrylic paint/coloured card
- Scissors

1

Paint the inside of your box black with acrylic paint, indluding the lid if it has one. Let the paint dry thoroughly before moving on to the next step.

2

Place your magnifying glass flat against one of the short sides of your box. Draw around the magnifying glass to create a circle in the centre.

3

Ask an adult to help!

Cut out the circle you drew, being careful not to go outside the line or your circle may end up too big. If you're using a craft knife, ask an adult.

4

Place your magnifying glass over the hole, on the inside of the box. Glue the magnifying glass in place, but don't get any glue on the lens itself!

5

Use the aluminium wire to make a phone stand. Start by bending the back rest section – this should be about as high as your phone is wide.

6

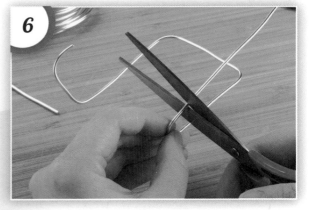

Bend the wire out on either side to make legs. Make them short, to keep your phone upright. Curve the ends up to hold the phone in place.

7

Try your phone in the stand and adjust it slightly until it holds your phone up like this. Make it as upright as you can without the phone falling over.

Locking your phone orientation

When the lens focuses the light from the screen onto a wall, it will also turn the image upside down (see p33). To make sure you can see it correctly, you'll need to lock your phone orientation in the settings menu, then place the phone upside down in the box when you're projecting.

8

Now make a lens ring to decorate the front of your projector. First trace a circle the same size as the one you cut out of the box.

9

Draw a circle about 2cm wider around it, then cut it out. Remove the space in the smaller circle to create a ring.

10

Use your glue gun to attach the ring to the outside of your box.

How it works

The lens inside a magnifying glass is convex, meaning it is thicker in the middle and has thinner edges. This allows it to gather and bend light.

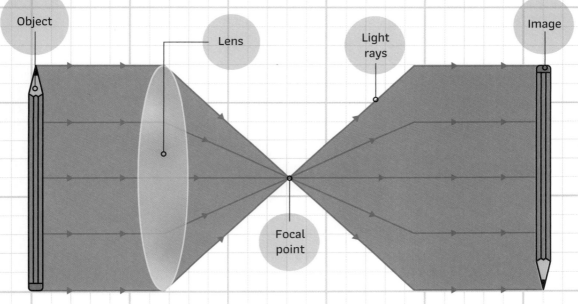

Object

Lens

Light rays

Image

Focal point

As the light from your phone hits the lens, it bends and is then concentrated to a single point, called a focus point.

As the beams of light pass through the focus point, they cross, causing the image to flip upside down.

This crystal ball works in a similar way to a lens – the light is bent as it travels through the inside of the glass, so the image you see is upside down.

18 Use paints and coloured card to decorate the outside of your projector – we've chosen a funky star theme.

12

Place your phone and stand at the other of the box. Adjust the stand so the screen faces the lens, so it can project through it.

The darker the room, the brighter your phone projection will appear!

How to use your projector

1. Turn the brightness on your phone up to its maximum, and lock your screen in an upside down position.

2. You want the image on your phone to be upside down so that when it is projected through the lens it will be flipped the right way up.

3. Place the phone on its wire stand inside the box and turn out the lights in the room. Face your projector towards a flat surface such as a wall and your image will appear.

4. Experiment with moving the phone closer to or further away from the lens until the image appears sharper and clearer.

The Science of
Sound and vision

Mirrors & reflection

Normally when we look in a mirror we only see one reflection. When you place two mirrors at an angle of less than 180 degrees, an object is reflected multiple times. The smaller the angle, the more times the object is reflected.

Try it at home
Take two small mirrors and tape them together to form a hinge. Place an object in front of the mirrors. See how many reflections you can make by slowly moving the mirrors together.

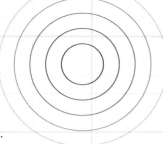

How the eye works

The human eye works a bit like your photo projector. Your eyeball is a ball with a hole in the front, called a pupil, to let light in. Behind this is a curved lens which bends and focuses the light onto the retina at the back of the eye.

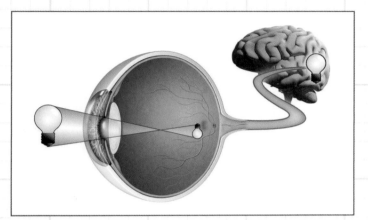

So how come we don't see everything upside-down, like in your projector? Behind the retina are hundreds of thousands of light-sensitive cells that send the picture to the brain through the optic nerve. Our super-clever brain then flips the picture so it is the right way up!

The science of sound

Sound is an incredible force! It is produced when two objects hit each other, causing a vibration. Sound can only travel through either a solid, liquid or gas, so in space where there is a vacuum, there is no sound. Sound is carried in waves, and the different sized waves will determine the type of sound we hear. The smaller the sound wave, the quieter the sound is and the closer the waves are together, the higher the pitch.

Blasting rocks with sound!
Did you know you can smash stone with the power of sound? People who suffer from kidney stones might undergo a medical procedure called extracorporeal shock wave lithotripsy. A machine is used to produce high frequency sound waves. These waves travel through the body and into the kidney stones. The vibrations cause the stones to crumble and break into tiny pieces. This then travels out of the body in the patients' wee!

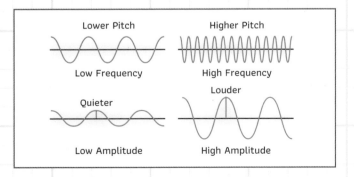

Lower Pitch

Higher Pitch

Low Frequency

High Frequency

Quieter

Louder

Low Amplitude

High Amplitude

Wearables

Get creative with these marvellous
makes that you can wear!

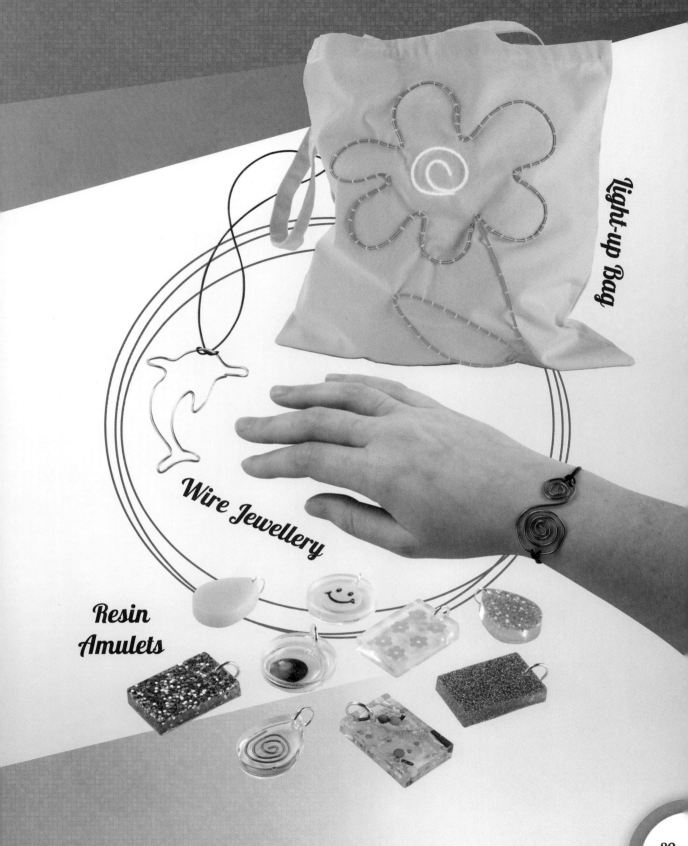

Light-up Bag

Wire Jewellery

Resin
Amulets

39

Light-up Bag

Stitch fantastic, flexible electroluminescent wire into crazy shapes to decorate a bag that actually lights up when you switch it on!

You will need...

Needle and thread

EL wire with battery pack (3 metres in whichever colours you like best)

Plain bag

Water-soluble transfer pen

2 x AA batteries

Plus...

- Pencil
- Scissors
- Paper

1

Use your paper and pencil to draw out your idea, making sure it will fit on to your bag. Simple designs work best! Erase any mistakes with water.

2

Ask an adult to help!

Make a small hole where you want to start your design, using the scissors. Make sure it is just big enough for your wire to fit through.

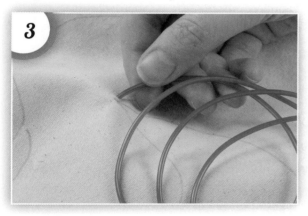

3

Pull your EL wire through the hole from the inside of your bag to the outside, so all of the EL wire is on the outside and the battery pack is inside.

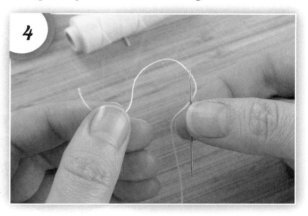

4

Thread your needle with the white thread, tying a knot in the end. You can use this to sew your EL wire onto the bag, following the design.

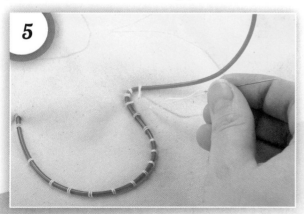

5

Starting 5cm from the hole, stitch across the EL wire, as close to either side of the it as possible. Make more stitches every few centimetres.

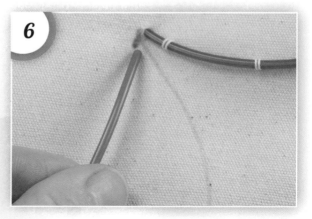

6

Repeat this process the whole way along. Make your stitches closer together on curves, to make sure the EL wire stays where you want it.

7

When you reach the end of your design, make another small hole and feed any remaining EL wire through, so it's on the inside of your bag.

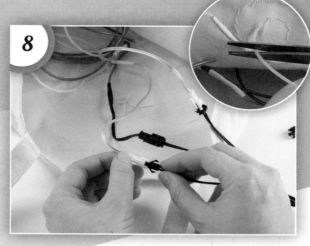

8

Trim any excess EL wire and seal the end with electrical tape. Connect each wire to the battery pack. Turn on the pack, and you're ready to glow!

How it works

Your light-up bag design uses electroluminescent wire ['EL wire' for short]. This is a thin wire made up of a conductive copper core which is coated in a thin layer of phosphor, a substance that illuminates when an electric current is passed through it.

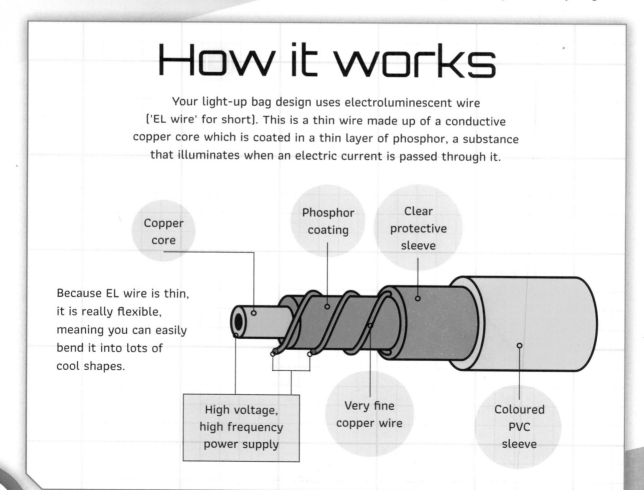

Copper core

Phosphor coating

Clear protective sleeve

Because EL wire is thin, it is really flexible, meaning you can easily bend it into lots of cool shapes.

High voltage, high frequency power supply

Very fine copper wire

Coloured PVC sleeve

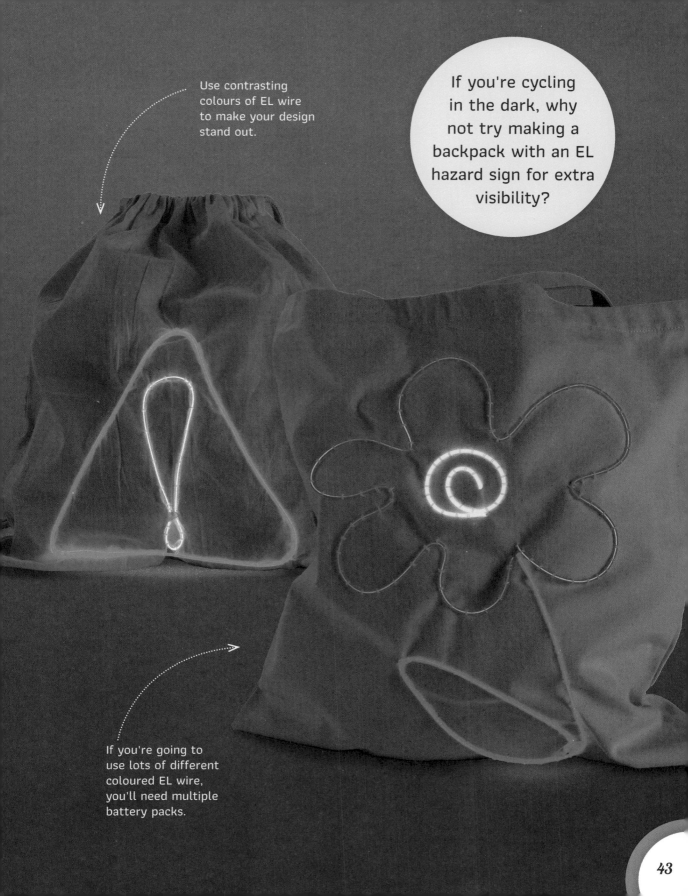

Use contrasting colours of EL wire to make your design stand out.

If you're cycling in the dark, why not try making a backpack with an EL hazard sign for extra visibility?

If you're going to use lots of different coloured EL wire, you'll need multiple battery packs.

Wire Jewellery

Let your imagination run wild and create colourful wire shapes that can be easily turned into jewellery or hanging decorations.

Round nosed jewellery pliers

Copper or aluminium wire – in as many colours as you like

Thin leather or faux leather cord

Plus...

• Sharp scissors
• Paper
• Pen
• Pencil

44

1

Use paper and pencils to draw out your design, or use one of the templates on the next page. Don't forget to plan where you'll attach the cord.

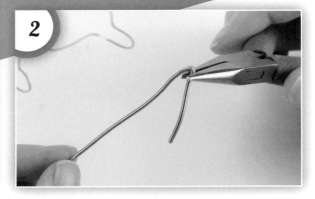

2

Use your pliers to bend your wire to the shape you have drawn. Take your time – if you need to, you can always flatten it out and start again.

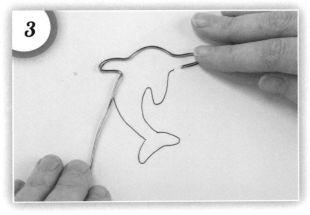

3

For tricky parts and sharp corners, you might need to lay the wire flat onto your design and follow the line exactly.

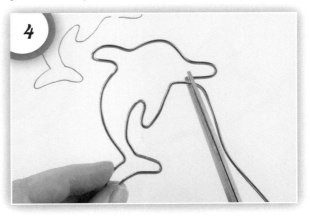

4

Once you're happy with the shape you have made, use sharp scissors to cut the wire at the end of your piece.

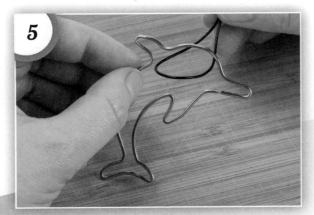

5

To make a bracelet, cut two pieces of cord 30cm each. Fold the first piece in half. Insert the folded piece of cord through the wire shape.

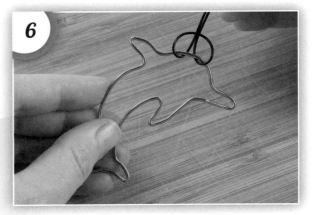

6

Pull the unfolded end of the cord through the loop, which will attach it to your wire. Repeat for the other side of the bracelet with the other cord.

Jewellery templates

Stars are a great first shape to try – make sure you use the template so that all the points are the same length.

When you're bending spiral shapes, start from the middle and work out.

Bend a second piece of wire across the leaf shape to add the central stalk for this design.

Why not make a necklace by attaching your design to one 45cm piece of cord?

Resin Amulets

Learn to cast with epoxy resin, and create fun colourful pieces you can turn into jewellery, keyrings, hanging decorations, or anything else you can think of.

You will need...

Small measuring jug

Coloured beads or shapes

Acrylic paint or alcohol inks

Jump rings

Two part epoxy resin

Glitter

Silicon jewellery keyring moulds

Plus...

- Plastic cups
- Wooden lolly sticks
- Disposable plastic gloves
- Necklace chain
- Jewellery pliers

1

2

Ask an adult to help!

You won't require much resin, but mixing resin in very small quantities can be quite tricky, so it's best to mix up more resin than you need.

Measure out the resin and hardener as precisely as possible, according to the ratio on the packaging. Stir really well for roughly three minutes.

Combining your resin

Making sure your resin and hardener are combined properly is very important, so set a timer for three minutes and keep stirring. As you stir, make sure to scrape the sides and bottom of the cup so everything is incorporated and you don't have any mixture stuck to the edges. Any resin stuck to the sides and bottom wont be able to catalyse properly, and won't harden.

3

4

Once your resin is properly mixed, you can add colour or glitter. If you want your resin to be a solid colour, you can use acrylic paint to colour it.

Add one drop at a time, stirring continuously. Don't add too much, as this can affect the chemical reaction. For a transparent effect, use alcohol ink.

5

Pour the resin into the moulds. You can use a wooden lolly stick to scoop resin into the mould rather than pouring it.

6

Leave your moulds for 24-48 hours on a flat smooth surface. Once your resin has cured, it is time to demould your pieces. Carefully peel back the silicon moulds to reveal your jewellery.

Filling the Moulds

Add your resin to the mould slowly to help prevent air bubbles forming. If you do notice air bubbles appearing, gently blow on the surface of your resin to help pop them. Be careful not to overfill your mould – the resin should sit level with the top of the mould. If you do overfill your mould, just scoop a little of the resin back into the cup and wipe any spills with a dry piece of kitchen towel.

How it works

Epoxy resin is made up of two parts. An epoxy, which is a highly reactive substance and a hardener or catalyst. When the hardener is added to the epoxy, a chemical reaction takes place. This reaction is exothermic, meaning heat is produced. This heat sets the resin in a process called curing. Epoxy resins are often used as super strong adhesives.

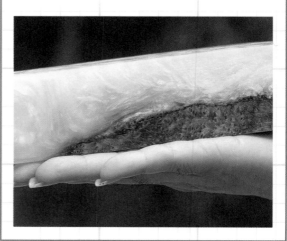

7

You can now turn your resin pieces into wearable jewellery. Take a jump ring, and carefully open it using jewellery pliers.

8

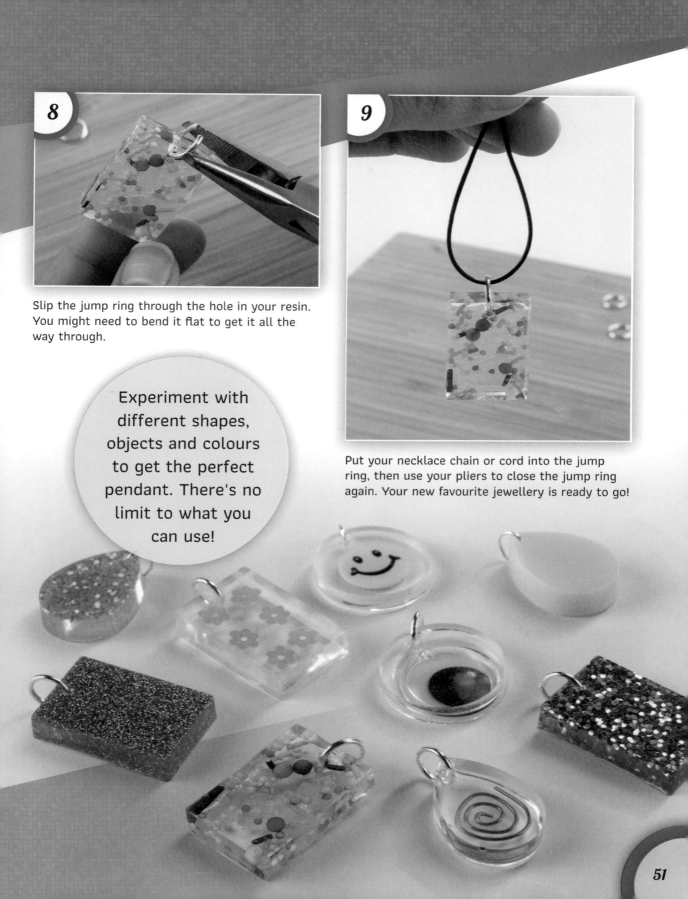

Slip the jump ring through the hole in your resin. You might need to bend it flat to get it all the way through.

Experiment with different shapes, objects and colours to get the perfect pendant. There's no limit to what you can use!

9

Put your necklace chain or cord into the jump ring, then use your pliers to close the jump ring again. Your new favourite jewellery is ready to go!

The Science of
Wearables

Wearable tech

We are seeing more and more wearable tech inventions, from smart watches and light up frocks, to fitness trackers and smart headphones. One of the most 'James Bond' types of tech has got to be Smart Glasses! These allow you to take pictures or to see virtual objects, images and data right in your line of sight. So you could play your favourite video game on your dining room table, get real-time directions as you walk down the street, or even have a 3D chat with someone who is hundreds of miles away, but appears to be standing in your room.

Verdigris

Your copper wire might be coloured, but did you know that copper changes colour all by itself? When copper is exposed to oxygen in the air, a chemical reaction takes place and bright green copper oxide is formed. It's called verdigris and is the reason New York's Statue of Liberty is green – the statue is actually made of copper. You can see the same effect on old copper coins, too.

Resin teeth

Have you ever had a filling at the dentist? Dentists often use composite resins to repair broken teeth or full cavities. A small amount is used as glue or a filler and it's set with light instead of heat! A small handheld blue light is used to cure the resin. The energy from the light waves causes a chemical reaction to take place, making the resin set hard.

At Home

These funky projects can bring your family pictures to life and even brighten up your bathtime!

Colour Change
Bath Bombs

Animated
Picture Frame

55

Colour Change Bath Bombs

You will need...

Witch hazel water spray

Create sparkling crystal decorations to hang around your home using a solution of Borax and water. Watch crystals form and grow as if by magic!

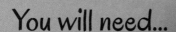

Powdered cosmetic pigment

Moulds

Mixing bowls and spoon

Citric Acid

Sodium bicarbonate

Plus...

• Disposable gloves
• Kitchen scales
• A nice warm bath!

In the mixing bowl, combine 300g of sodium bicarbonate and 100g of citric acid.

Add a teaspoon of your chosen pigment at a time, until you have a colour you're happy with.

Spray lightly with witch hazel water. Mix well using your hands, being sure to wear disposable gloves to avoid the pigment staining your skin.

The mixture should have the consistency of wet sand – it should hold together when squeezed. If it's too dry, add a few more sprays of witch hazel.

Fill the two halves of the small bath bomb moulds with the mixture, pressing it down to make sure it's nice and compact.

Place two halves together, and push tightly. Remove one half of the mould, but leave the bath bomb in the other half for at 30 minutes.

How it works

1. When you drop your bath bomb into water, a chemical reaction takes place, producing the fizz.

2. As the first layer dissolves, the pigment colours your bath water.

3. Once the outer layer has completely dissolved, the reaction will start on the different coloured core.

4. As this new colour mixes with the first, your bath water will begin to change colour.

7 Now combine 300g of sodium bicarbonate and 100g of citric acid. Add a different pigment, spray lightly with witch hazel, mix well and fill one large mould.

8 Loosely pack a small amount of mixture in the other half of the mould, and place your small bath bomb inside. Pack any gaps with the other mixture.

9

Tightly push the two halves together. Remove one half of the mould, but leave the bath bomb in the other half. Repeat with the remaining moulds.

10

Leave the bath bomb for 20-30 minutes before moving the other mould half. Your bath bombs are now ready to use!

Find your best colour combinations - the more different the two colours, the better.

Animated Picture Frame

Bring a favourite photo to life with this marvelous, mechanical animated picture frame.

You will need...

Cardboard

Two photographs — one of a background, and one of a person or pet

Scissors

Wooden dowels

Plus...

- Ruler
- Pencil
- Craft knife
- Glue gun
- Side cutters

1 Measure and cut out two pieces of cardboard that are 19cm by 12cm, and two pieces that are 17cm by 12cm.

2 Measure a 2cm strip along the 12cm edge on each of your cardboard pieces. Score along this line so that you have a folded end.

3 Assemble a rectangular box shape using these pieces – the two shorter pieces will be the sides and the longer pieces will be the top and bottom.

4 Use your glue gun to put glue along the outside of the 2cm folded strip, and attach this to the inside of the next piece.

5 Draw and cut two 7cm-wide circles from cardboard. These will become the parts for the mechanism.

6 Mark the centre point on one of your circles, and then make a hole slightly off-centre, using a pencil.

Use a glue gun to add two cardboard strips to the
other circle, about 2cm apart.

Cut down your second wooden dowel until it's
roughly 10cm long.

Make a hole in the top of your box, directly above
where your cardboard circle is. Insert your piece
of wooden dowel through this hole.

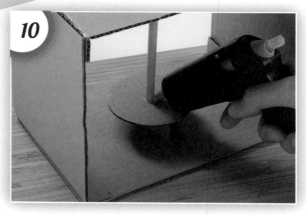

Now glue the circle with the card strips to the
bottom of the dowel.

Glue two more card strips on either side of the
dowel, lengthways across the inside top of the box.

Cut out four 5cm triangular pieces cardboard
pieces, and glue them to each corner to stabilise
your frame.

13

Insert the other dowel through the hole in the side, then through the hole in your cardboard circle, and then out the other side of the box.

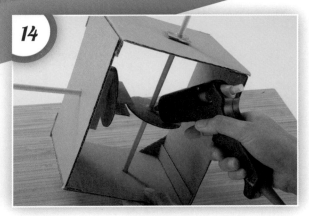

14

Position your dowel so the circle sits between the two strips of card, then carefully glue the circle to the dowel.

15

Cut a 5cm square of cardboard, pierce it with the dowel and glue in place outside the box, making sure the dowel can still turn.

16 From your cardboard cut a piece measuring 17cm by 11cm. Glue your background photo to this piece of cardboard and trim off any excess. Cut out your person or pet photograph and glue it to the end of the vertical wooden dowel.

Turn the handle to make your front picture bob up and down!

The Science of
At Home

Colour changing science

Have you ever had a hot drink from a colour changing mug? As you pour in a hot drink, the cup changes colour and reveals a new colour. But what is actually happening? These mugs use a technology called thermochromic ink. This means that the ink materials change their colour depending on the temperature. Leuco dyes are special dyes that can change their chemical form depending on how warm it is. These are used in heat changing mugs as a top layer that can change from a dark colour to transparent, revealing a picture beneath. Thermochromic inks are also used in thermometers, cars, baby bottles and loads more cool things.

Mechanical marvels

Mechanical toys (or automata) like your animated photo frame have been around for a very long time. The earliest examples were made by the Ancient Greeks. Hero of Alexandria was a famous Greek mathematician who made many mechanical devices. One of his most famous was a water basin with a metal bird that sang and an owl that would turn and make the birds go quiet. Hero also invented the first automatic door around 2000 years ago!

How it works

The card disks used in your animated frame are a special type of mechanical disk called a cam. It's a bit like a funny-shaped wheel. If it is a round cam, instead of having a hole in the centre like wheels do, it is offset to one side. This causes the cam to rise up and down as it spins on its axe. This motion can then be used to drive an object up and down.

Sleeve   Follower

Driven axle

Pear-shaped cam   Snail cam   Eccentric cam

Outdoors

With these fun, useful projects, you can record the weather, feed birds or even bring the outdoors inside!

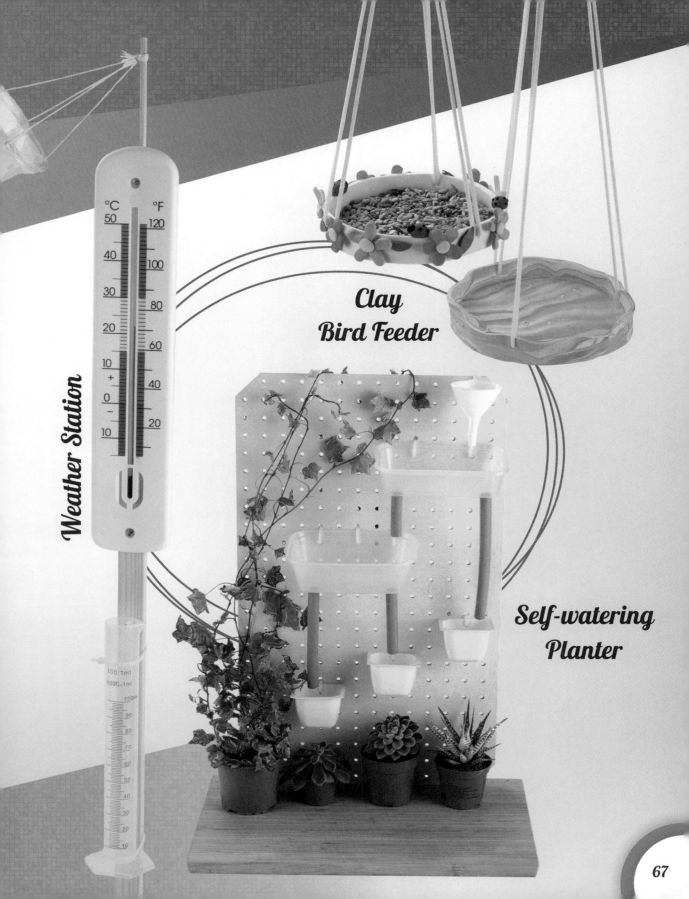

Weather Station

Clay
Bird Feeder

Self-watering
Planter

Weather Station

Have you ever wanted to be a meteorologist? Record the weather in your area with this weather station and report board.

Split pins

Cable ties

Measuring cylinder

Outdoor thermometer

Self-adhesive velcro

Wooden dowel

String

Plastic bag

Coloured card

Plus...

- Foam board (A2 size)
- White card
- Permanent marker pen
- Scissors
- Glue gun
- Pencil
- Ruler
- Craft knife
- Lollipop stick
- 2mm aluminium wire
- Large plastic bowl
- 1m wooden stick

68

1

Start by preparing a wind sock. Lay the plastic bag flat, cut off the handles, then cut off the bottom where the bag is sealed.

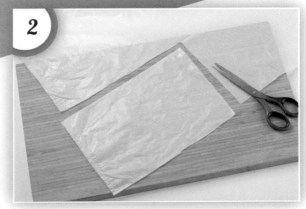

2

Cut up one side of your bag, open it out flat and cut out a long rectangle of plastic.

3

Form a ring roughly 8cm wide using your aluminium wire. Double up the wire to give it a bit more strength.

4

Glue around the outside edge of the wire, then wrap your strip of plastic bag around it, leaving a 2cm flap at the top of the strip.

5

Glue the flap to the inside of the wire ring, to completely cover the wire. Make the plastic into a tube by gluing it together along the long end.

Make four evenly spaced holes through the plastic, just above the ring. Thread four lengths of string through the holes, tying a knot on the inside to secure them in place. Tie the strings to a wooden dowel, roughly 5cm from the end.

How it works

Your weather station is made up of these three components.

① WIND SOCK
This light plastic sock will be blown by even light breezes, allowing you to see which direction the wind is blowing.

② THERMOMETER
The thermometer will allow you to read the outdoor temperature, measured in celsius or fahrenheit.

RAIN GAUGE
This collects rain, and will allow you to measure how much rain has fallen within one 24-hour period.

③

④ EXTRA COMPONENT: BAROMETER
If you want to record the air pressure, you could even add a barometer to your station! This device measures air pressue and can help you predict when storms are on their way – air always moves from areas of high pressure to low.

Assemble your three elements on your stick like this to create your outdoor weather station.

Fix the windsock pole to the top of the stick with wood glue or small nails.

°C   °F
50   120
40   100
30   80
20   60
10
 +   40
 0
 –   20
10

Screw your thermometer in place, or use zip ties and glue to fix it onto the stick.

If you don't have the right sized stick, you could always secure the components to a wooden board instead.

14

To make the report board, cut a piece of 300mm x 90mm green card, red card measuring 200mm x 200mm, and a 130mm x 95mm piece of blue card. Add self-adhesive velcro to each panel.

15

To create your wind direction dial, cut out a circle and an arrow shape. Use a split pin to attach them to the foam board. Add the coloured card to the foam board, as shown on page 75.

Use zip ties to fix your measuring cylinder in place, making sure that the top isn't covered so rain can fall into it.

100:1ml
In20C±1ml
100ml
90
80
70
60
50
40
30
20
10

How to use your weather station

Place your weather station outside in an exposed spot and find out the directions of North, East, South and West using a compass.

Note down which way the wind is blowing, the temperature and the amount of rainfall collected in the beaker, and then display these results on your chart.

Try to check your weather station at the same time each day.

Don't forget to empty the cylinder after recording the amount of rainfall.

If you enter the daily weather results into a spreadsheet, you can start to see patterns in the data. Can you work out the total rainfall for March? Or how much hotter August is than December?

Make two holes and tie some string to the board so you can hang it in your room!

WEATHER REPORT

TODAY'S DATE IS

| MONDAY | 8TH | AUGUST |

THE WEATHER IS

SUNNY

AND

WINDY

RAINFALL

3mm

WIND

N
W   E
S

TEMPERATURE

-5   0   5   10   15   20   25   30   35

Clay Bird Feeder

You will need...

How many different types of bird are there in your area? Make your own bird feeder and see how many birds you can spot using it.

Cotton cord

Wooden ring

Polymer clay in your choice of colours

Rolling pin

Pencil

E6000 glue

Plus...

- Table knife
- Ruler
- Baking tray
- Greaseproof paper

1

Choose a clay colour for the main dish part of the bird feeder. Roll this out, using your rolling pin, into a rough circle that's about 3mm thick.

2

Find a round object (or make a card template) that's the same size as you want your bird feeder to be. Place it on the clay, and cut around it.

3

Take another piece of clay and roll it out into a long narrow tube, slightly longer than the circumference of your circle.

4

Now use a rolling pin to flatten it so it's roughly 1.5cm wide.

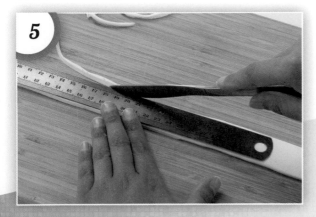

5

Use your ruler and craft knife to trim the edges of the strip so they are flat.

6

Stand your clay strip up, and begin wrapping it around the outside of the base, pushing the two together so they are nice and snug.

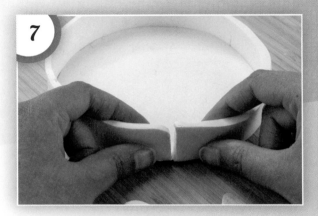

Trim off any excess clay from your strip, then press together where the start and end of your strip meet, until no join is visible.

Make three holes in the clay strip for the hanging cord. Space the holes out equally, using a ruler to ensure they are the same distance from the rim.

Mixing colours

To get a marble effect, roll a second colour of clay into a thinner tube. Wind it around your main piece of clay, then roll it back into a ball. Roll it out again, and your clay will be 'marbled' with the new colour.

Cut petals and leaves from clay using a craft knife. If they aren't perfect, you can shape them more with your hands once you've cut them out.

Once all your components have been made, it's time to bake them. Take your baking tray and cover it with greaseproof paper.

11

Ask an adult to help!

Lay all your pieces right way up on the tray. Preheat your oven to the temperature for your brand of clay. Bake for the recommended time.

12

Remove from the overn and allow to cool. Attach your clay pieces around the sides of your bird feeder using E6000 glue.

13

Cut three 1m pieces of cord. Thread each piece through one of the holes, and pull it through so it's halfway through.

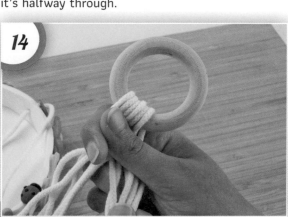

14

Bring all your pieces of cord up to the centre above your bird feeder, and attach to your wooden ring. This will allow you to hang up your bird feeder.

Try and find a sheltered spot to hang your feeder from – under a tree or against a wall or fence will be ideal.

Self-watering Planter

Combine recycling and water dynamics to create a plant watering system that will keep your houseplants happy and healthy.

You will need...

Piece of pegboard measuring approx 40cm by 60cm

Plastic flexible piping

Plastic funnel and foam and container

Paint

Empty plastic containers x2 larger and x2 smaller

Plus...

- Paint brush
- Long cable ties
- Bradawl
- Glue gun
- Craft knife
- Hot glue gun

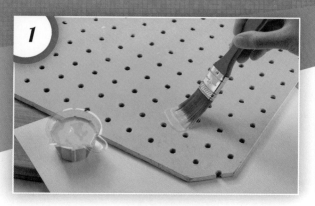

Start by painting your pegboard. We painted ours with a base coat of white and then two coats of yellow. Allow to dry completely.

Stuff the end of the funnel with the foam, so water can drip through slowly. Cut four pieces of piping measuring 6cm, 10cm, 16cm and 19cm.

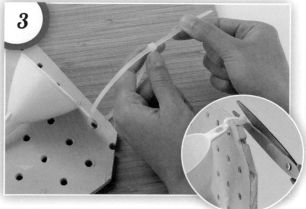

Attach your funnel to the top right of your pegboard using a cable tie.

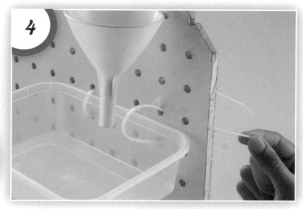

Make two or three holes along one long side of the container. Use these to attach the container under the funnel with cable ties.

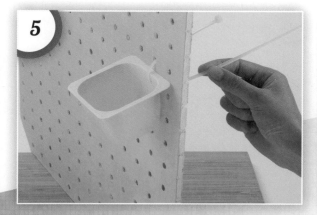

Make a hole in one side of each of your smaller plastic containers and use this to attach each of them to your pegboard using a cable tie.

Take the larger container and make a hole at either end in the bottom using your bradawl.

How it works

Cable ties, sometimes called zip ties, are made of a flexible plastic called nylon. They are made up of a long length covered in tiny teeth. The thin pointy end is threaded into the ratchet at the other end and pulled to tighten. The sloping shape of the teeth mean the cable tie can only get tighter and cannot be undone.

Some zip ties are so strong, they are even used as handcuffs!

7

Glue the 6cm and 19cm piping to the holes in the container, as shown on page 83. Repeat steps 5-8 with the other large container, lower down.

8

Using a bradawl, make five small holes in the bottom of each of your smaller containers. This will allow the water to sprinkle over your plants.

Position your plants underneath each pot, then fill up the funnel with water and watch it drip down!

The Science of
Outdoors

Every wondered why some storms or severe weather get given names, or how they decide what to call a storm? Severe weather around the world that might cause danger to life, such as tornados, hurricanes or major storms, is given a name to help avoid confusion and to aid communication. Names are given by the region where the storm originates, and alternate from male to female names in alphabetical order.

Bird super-senses

You may spot pigeons feeding from your bird feeder... but did you realise how amazing they are? Homing pigeons use highly attuned senses to find their way back home, no matter how far away they are. They were even used to carry secret messages from behind enemy lines in the First and Second World Wars. So how do these super-navigators find their way back to their nests from thousands of miles away? Recent research suggests that pigeons use ultra low frequency sound waves that emit from the landscape to form a mental map. They use this map, and familiar landmarks, to find their way home.

Hydroponics

What do your plants need to grow? Water, sunshine and soil, right? Well, actually no! They don't really need soil, just the nutrients that the soil contains. Plants can be grown using hydroponics, a system where the roots of the plant are submersed in water. Nutrients are then added to the water to feed the plants. Some growers have taken hydroponics to the next level and use a system called aquaponics. Instead of adding nutrients to the water, fish are kept in tanks along side the plants and the fish poo feeds the plants!

Decorations

Use science and tech principles to create these wonderful decorations for your home.

Crystal Hanging Decorations

Rainbow Jar Light

DO
NOT
DISTURB!

Crystal Hanging Decorations

You will need...

Create sparkling crystal decorations to hang around your home using a solution of borax and water. Watch as crystals form and grow as if by magic. How big can you get your crystals to grow?

String

Borax powder

Hot water and tablespoon

Plus...
- Hot water
- String
- Craft sticks

Coloured pipe cleaners

86

Start by bending your pipe cleaners into whatever shapes you'd like your decorations to be. You can even join together two pipe cleaners if you like.

Tie a length of string to the top of your pipe cleaner shape. This will be your hanging loop, so make sure it's long enough.

We tied our hanging string to a lolly stick to keep the decoration suspended, but you can use whatever you have handy (a pencil works well!)

Pour two cups of very hot water from the kettle into the jar.

Dissolve 6 tablespoons of the borax powder, stirring well until all of the powder has dissolved. Pour the borax solution into your glass jars or bowls. Make sure you have a separate bowl or jar for each of your decorations because you don't want them to touch each other while the crystals are forming.

How it works

Crystals are groups of atoms that connect together in a repeating pattern. Different types of crystals have different shapes. Salt is a cube shaped crystal and quartz is hexagonal.

Lots of materials are made up of crystalline structures, including metal and even chocolate! Snowflakes are always six-sided crystals, but amazingly, each one is different from the next.

The molecules in snowflakes join together in a hexagonal structure, leading to six-sided flakes.

When viewed under a microscope, it's easy to see that salt is made of perfect cubic crystals.

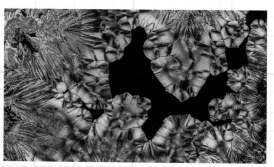

Vitamin C forms crystals when it reacts with the oxygen in the air.

6

Give the borax solution another stir. You can make more solution if you need to by doubling or tripling these quantities.

7

Suspend your decoration in the solution, making sure the pipe cleaners aren't touching the sides or bottom of the jar.

8 Leave your decorations in the borax solution for at least three hours for the crystals to start to form. For the best crystals, we recommend leaving them in overnight. Then you can remove them carefully from the jar and find somewhere to hang your amazing crystal decorations!

Crystal growing

If crystals haven't formed after 24 hours, don't panic. Sometimes they need a little bit longer – check them again after an extra 12 or 24 hours and crystals should have formed. The longer you leave them in the borax solution, the longer the crystals have to grow!

Rainbow Jar Light

Liquids with different densities will float on each other. Use this to create a beautiful rainbow light display whose colours seem to float magically!

You will need...

Foil tape

Used tape roll

LED light

Battery pack

2 x AA batteries

Glass jar with cork lid

Plus...

- Pencils
- Thin white card
- Scissors
- Spoons
- Hot glue gun
- Food colouring

- 150ml honey
- 150ml hand soap
- 150ml water
- 150ml olive oil
- 150ml surgical spirit

First, draw two circles around the tape roll on a sheet of thin white card.

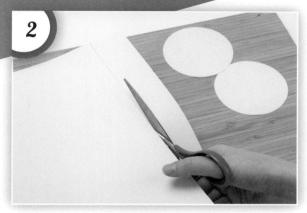

Now cut out a 40mm wide strip of card, long enough to go all the way around your jar.

Ask an adult to help!

Cut out the card circles and make a 1cm hole in the centre of one of them.

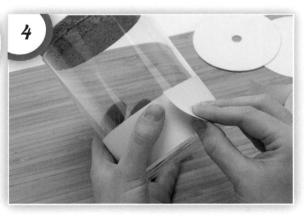

Wrap the strip of card around the jar and stick the ends together, but don't glue or tape it to the jar.

Glue the card circle with the hole to the bottom of your jar.

Form the base of the jar by gluing the other card circle to the bottom of the tape roll.

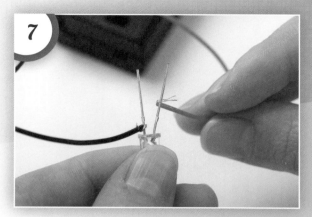

Connect the LED to the battery pack, making sure that the red wire is connected to the longer of the LED's pins.

Insert the battery pack, then glue the LED to the top so it's right in the centre of the jar.

Join the card ring to the tape roll with the foil tape, making sure the card sticks up by 5cm.

The jar should sit snugly in the base, but still let you take it out to access the battery pack.

Now make your liquids! Add purple food colouring to your 150ml of honey and mix well.

Pour it slowly and carefully into the bottom of your jar, making sure you don't touch the sides.

Mix the hand soap with blue colouring and pour it on top. Be super slow and careful so the two liquids don't mix!

Add green food colouring to the water, then pour it in very slowly, so it sits on top of the soap.

Add the olive oil (this doesn't need any colouring!) slowly so it floats on top of the water.

Finally, colour your surgical spirit red and add it to the top of the jar.

Remove the jar and switch on the LED for an amazing display - but be careful not to mix the liquids!

Solar Powered Door Sign

Jazz up your bedroom door with this funky whiteboard sign, illuminated with lights that only shine in the dark!

You will need...

Wood

Sandpaper

Paint brush

Wood glue

Acrylic paint

Solar powered fairy lights

Plus...

- Drill
- 6mm wood drill bit
- Whiteboard card
- Pencil
- Ruler
- Glue gun
- Dry-erase marker pens

1

Start by cutting your wood to the correct length, to make your frame.

Ask an adult to help!

2

Cut two pieces that are 225mm long, and two pieces that are 310mm long.

3

Sand down any edges until they rest snugly against the surface of the other piece of wood.

4

Glue one shorter piece to the edge of one of the longer pieces to form an 'L' shape. Repeat with the other two pieces of wood.

Fitting check

You can check if you have the pieces positioned correctly by holding a piece of A4 paper up to the gap in the frame. If it fits perfectly over the space then you have them positioned correctly.

5

Once the 'L' shapes have dried, glue them together to form a rectangular frame. The long piece should be glue against the side of the shorter piece on the opposite 'L' shape, NOT against the cut end of the shorter piece.

6

Using your ruler and pencil, mark a line along the centre of each strip of wood that makes up the frame.

Then mark evenly spaced points along this line, where you will be drilling holes for your fairy lights to poke through.

7

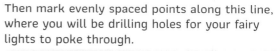

Ask an adult to help!

Drill carefully through your wood at the points you marked. Make sure your holes are straight, and that your lights can fit through the holes.

8

Paint your frame in your chosen colour. Give it several coats to get a nice finish. Don't forget to paint the inside and outside edges of the frame.

How it works

Solar powered lights are a great way to brighten up your projects and use an environmentally friendly source of power.

Photovoltaic cells absorb sunlight and transform it into energy that we can use to power our electrical devices. Most solar powered lights also contain a small battery, meaning energy can be collected in the day and emitted when it is dark.

Sunlight

Anti-reflective coating

Glass cover

Sunlight knocks electrons free

Conductor

Free electrons move to create electric current

Solar panels work by sandwiching layers of silicon under a transparent pane. When sunlight hits the silicon, it allows electrons to move between the layers, creating an electric current.

Solar powered lights like this garden light also contain a light sensor, which only completes the circuit when it's dark. This means that the lights won't come on until it's dark outside.

9

Don't worry if the lights are a bit loose – you can wrap a small piece of masking tape around the bottom of the light to keep it snug in the hole.

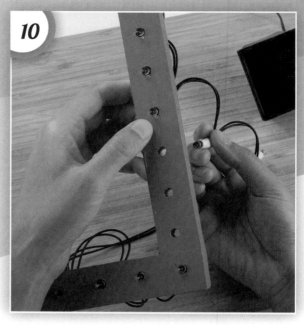

10

Allow your paint to dry completely, and then insert your lights into the holes.

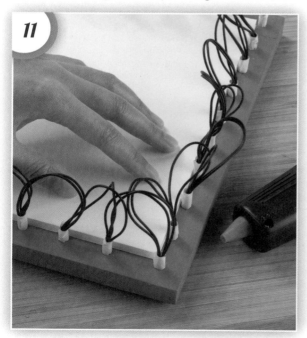

11

Flip your frame over an apply a line of hot glue around the inside edge of the frame. Press down your piece of whiteboard card.

12

Turn on your lights and your sign is ready for you to draw or write on - make sure you only use dry-erase pens otherwise they may not wipe off!

You can change your message to whatever you want, to match the situation or your mood!

The Science of
Decorations

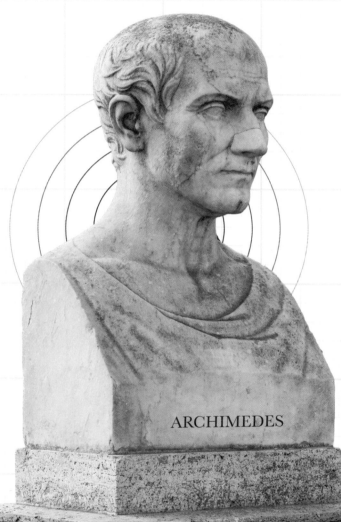

ARCHIMEDES

A famous ancient Greek scientist called Archimedes was asked by a king to find out if the goldsmith had stolen some gold when he made a new crown, and replaced it with some similar, cheaper metal. Archimedes went to have some quiet time in the bath to think about how he could answer this question. When he got in the full bath, his body displaced some of the water, causing it to spill out of the bath. It is said that Archimedes got out and ran through the town shouting "Eureka!", meaning "I've found it!". He realised that he could compare the densities of the metals by first displacing water to find the volume of an object, and then dividing the weight of the object by its volume to determine the density. We still use this equation today to work out the density of an object.

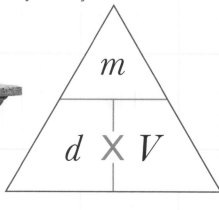

Diamonds

Diamonds are some of the most precious crystals on earth. Most diamonds we see were created millions of years ago, about 100 miles below the earth's surface. A combination of heat and pressure helped to turn carbon into these precious jewels. Diamonds are so hard, they are used to cut other very hard materials – including other diamonds. You can even buy drill bits with a diamond tip!

Can decorative lights improve our mood?

Well, it turns out that the answer is yes! Christmas lights and other light-up decorations can help cheer you up through something called chromotherapy. This is a scientific name for using coloured light to make us feel better, and we have been doing it for thousands of years! When we are feeling a little out of sorts, chromotherapy can use specific colours to help us improve our mood!

Glossary

Acetate
Clear plastic sheets, ideal for craft projects.

Aluminium wire
Thin, light, flexible wire, good for jewellery projects. Can be bought coated in multiple colours.

Automaton
Any machine that can be made to move like a living thing. The plural is 'automata'.

Axle
The revolving shaft connecting a set of wheels.

Bamboo skewers
Thin sticks with a pointy end made from bamboo. Used for making kebabs, but they make perfect lightweight axles too!

Borax powder
White powder, used to make crystals and slime.

Bradawl
A woodworking hand tool shaped a bit like a screwdriver with a pointed end.

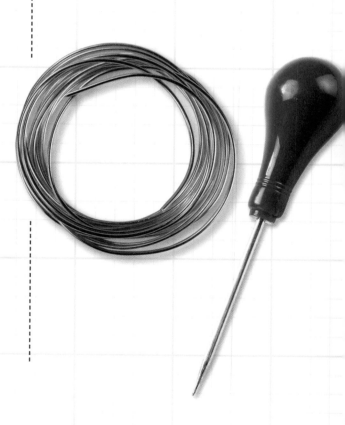

Citric acid

A weak acid that can be added to bath bombs to help them fizz.

Copper wire

Flexible metal wire which conducts electricity well.

Craft knife

Small knife with a retractable, replaceable blade.

Crystals

Regular structures whose shape is determined by the molecules they are made of.

Dowel

A long, thin cylindrical piece of wood – often used for when an axle is needed.

Electroluminescent (EL) wire

Flexible wire with that glows when an electrical current runs through it.

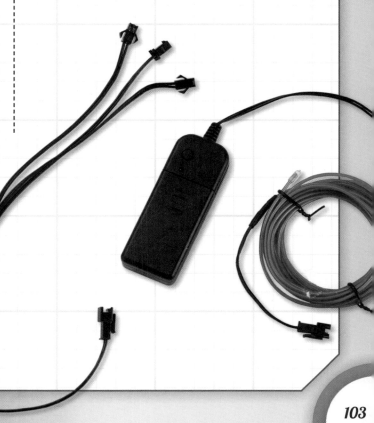

Epoxy resin

A clear solid which can be made by mixing resin with hardener.

Hand drill

A drill which is worked by turning a handle. Ideal for drilling through most craft materials.

Jewellery pliers

Small pliers of various types, used to bend wire or pick up small items.

Kaleidoscope

A tube that uses beads and mirrors to create an optical illusion.

LED

A light emitting diode is a semiconductor that emits light when electricity passes through it. A great energy-efficient light for electrical projects.

Silicon moulds

Reusable, flexible moulds which can be easily peeled away.

Sodium bicarbonate

Also known as baking soda, this powder fizzes in water when mixed with citric acid.

Thermometer

A mechanical or electronic device which allows you to read the temperature of its surroundings.

Verdigris

The green covering of copper carbonate or copper chloride that copper gets when exposed to the air.

Wind sock

Hollow tube which is light enough to rotate in the wind, allowing you to work out wind direction.

Witch hazel water

Water infused with the bark or leaves of the witch hazel tree.

Zip ties

Strong plastic single-use ties, perfect for securing two thin objects together.

Index

Your Notes

Use these pages to plan projects
or jot down new ideas.

flixngaant ix
bote and car r

hotoa

oser

hxed
witho

shot an

his fase.